LYNNE RAE PERKINS
THE BROKEN CAT

GREENWILLOW BOOKS
An Imprint of HarperCollinsPublishers

To Cam and Margie and Nasher
Lynne Rae Perkins

For all of the Franks, especially Frank P.

Thanks to Lucy, Frank, and Bill for their patience,
Lucy for the handwriting,
Frank for asking that question,
Dr. Peggy, Dr. Aunt Cookie, and Dr. Morrison,
and Virginia D.

The Broken Cat
Copyright © 2002 by Lynne Rae Perkins
All rights reserved.
Printed in Singapore by Tien Wah Press
www.harperchildrens.com

Pen and ink and watercolor paints were used for the full-color art.
The text type is Optima.

Library of Congress Cataloging-in-Publication Data

Perkins, Lynne Rae.
The broken cat / by Lynne Rae Perkins.
  p. cm.
"Greenwillow Books."
Summary: Andy asks his mother to tell the story about breaking her arm while
they wait for the veterinarian to determine what is wrong with their cat.
ISBN 0-06-029263-6 (trade). ISBN 0-06-029264-4 (lib. bdg.)
[1. Fractures—Fiction. 2. Cats—Fiction. 3. Wounds and injuries—Fiction.] I. Title.
PZ7.P4313 Th 2002   [E]—dc21   2001018780

1 2 3 4 5 6 7 8 9 10
First Edition

"Mom," said Andy, "can you tell me about that time when you were running because you were late for school and you tripped on a little chunk of sidewalk that was sticking up because of a tree root and you fell and broke your arm?"

"Let's see," said Andy's mom. "I think I was in second grade."

"No," said Andy's grandma,
"you were in the third grade."
"I must have been in the fifth
grade, then," said his aunt Cookie.
"Well, anyway," said his mom,
"it was a long time ago."

"Listen to this, Frank,"
Andy whispered
to his cat.

"A whole group of us
were walking to school.
We were almost down
the hill when we heard
the bell ring.
But was it the first
bell or the late bell?
No one was sure.

"We all started to run.
There were some huge
old trees all along
the way, and some of
their gnarly old roots
had broken and pushed
up hunks of the sidewalk.
I tripped on one and
went flying through the air.

"As I flew, I remembered that I was wearing my brand-new glasses. I flung my hands out so that I wouldn't land on my face and break them.

"It worked—when I crashed into the sidewalk, my glasses were saved. But the whole front of me was banged up and scraped and bruised, and my dress was torn."

"I wasn't very sympathetic," said Aunt Cookie. "I said, 'Stop whining and get up. We're late!'"

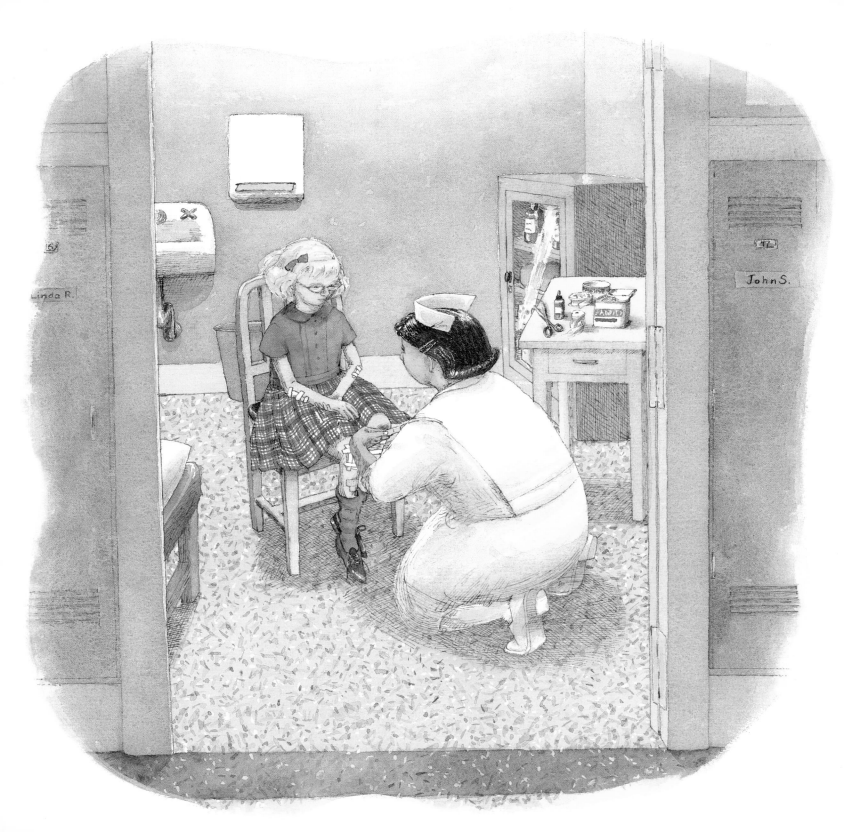

"The school nurse cleaned me up and bandaged me.
She asked if anything else hurt, but it was hard to tell.
Everything was stinging. So I said 'No,' and she sent
me back to class," said Andy's mom.

"That nurse felt so bad about not noticing that
your arm was broken," said Grandma. "Especially
when it was in the newspaper."

"Tell how you couldn't do your writing test,"
said Andy.

"I couldn't make my hand do what I wanted it
to do. But I still thought my arm was just sore.
I got a horrible grade.

"After school, I was supposed to
get ready for a birthday party.
But I couldn't pull my socks on."

"No, no, no," said Grandma.
"You couldn't get your socks
off to take a bath.

"And when you couldn't wash yourself, I called Liz to come over from next door to take a look. There was a lump where a watch would be, but on your right arm.

Oh, Helen, I think you better have someone take a look at that.

Look at that lump.

"So we went to the emergency room."

"I was wearing my dress for the party," said Andy's mom.
"I loved that dress. It was a hand-me-down from Aunt Cookie.
The top was peach with white rickrack and the bottom was
white with peach polka dots."

"I loved that dress, too," said Aunt Cookie.

"I was going to take you right from the hospital to the party,"
said Grandma. "That doctor was such a nice young man.
He was so gentle. You didn't cry a drop while he examined
your arm. Or while you got your X rays.

"When the nurse pinned up the X rays, I asked her,
'Do you think it's broken?' and she said, 'I'm not
supposed to tell you, but yes, it looks as if it's broken.'"
"And then did you cry and cry, and you couldn't
stop crying?" Andy asked his mom.

"I cried and cried, and I couldn't stop crying."

"Why did you cry so much?" asked Andy.

"I don't know—I think maybe I was just surprised
 that a part of me could break."

"You were sobbing," said Grandma. "I said,
'Settle down! You're going to get that nice
 nurse in trouble. She wasn't supposed to tell.'
 When the doctor came back, he said, 'What
 happened? What's wrong?' and you said,
'Oh, I'm just tired.'"

"I cried the whole time
he was putting on the
splint and the cast and
the sling. I wouldn't go
in to the birthday party,
even though they were
having pizza."
"You were embarrassed
that you were so late,"
said Grandma. "I carried
your gift up to the house."

"I was embarrassed
that my arm
was broken,"
said Andy's mom.
"I was embarrassed
that I was breakable."

"I was embarrassed because I had yelled at you,"
said Aunt Cookie. "Liz and I went around and told
everyone in the whole neighborhood that you had
gone to the hospital, and when you got home,
they all came out to greet you."

"Frank?" called out a voice.
Andy and his mother and his grandma and his aunt stood up and walked across the room.

They went into a smaller room, and Andy lifted
Frank up onto the tall, silvery table.
"It's okay," Andy whispered in his cat's ear.
"Hi, Frank," said the doctor. "What's the trouble?"

"He was fine yesterday morning,"
said Andy's mother.
"I let him outside," said Andy, "but
when he came back in, he crawled
up onto a chair, and he didn't move
all day."
"He wouldn't eat his supper or
drink any water," said Aunt Cookie.

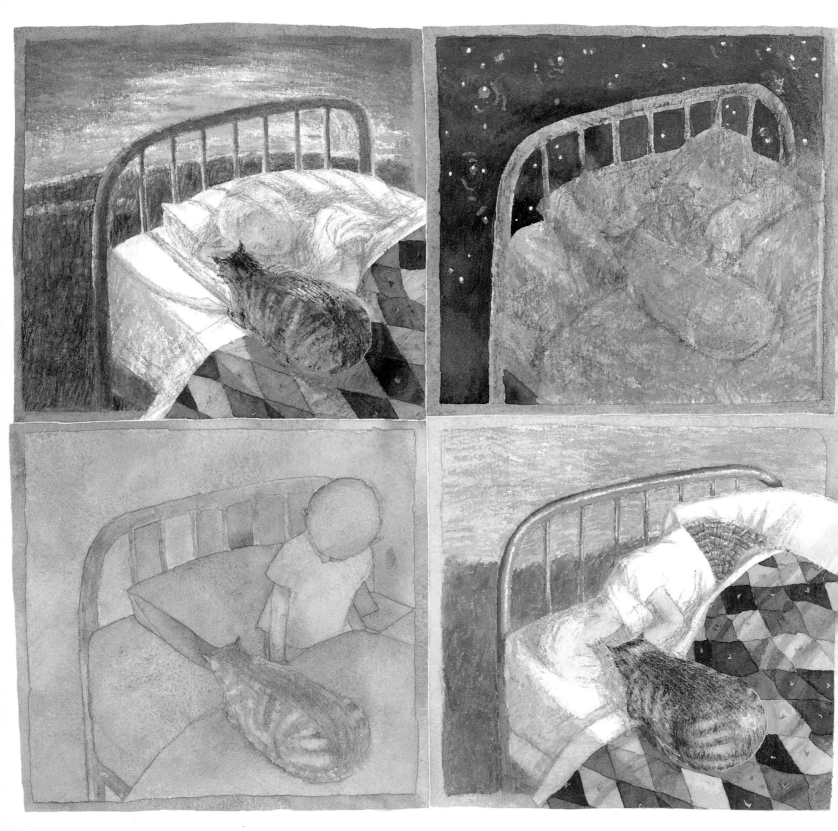

"I put him beside me on my bed," said Andy.
"He didn't move all night. I kept waking up
 and checking to see if he was still breathing."

"He seems to be squinching his eyes shut tight,"
 said Grandma.
"Hmm," said the doctor.

She searched Frank for clues. She took his temperature.
She pried open his eyes. She peeked into his mouth and
down his throat. She listened to the small noises Frank
made as her fingers felt his fur. It was as if she were a
fortune teller and Frank were her crystal ball.

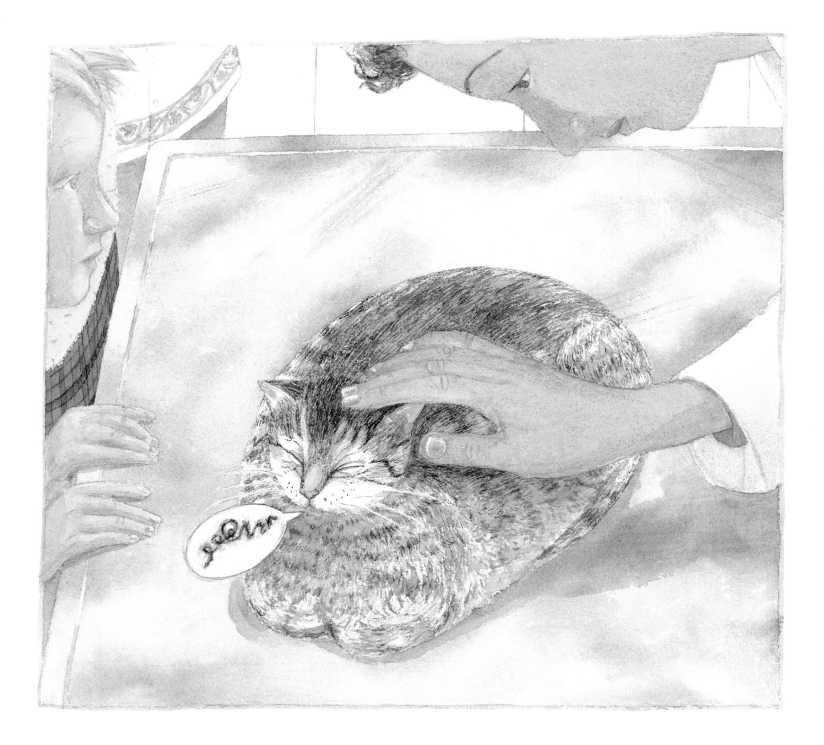

"It looks as if Frank may have been in a fight," she said. "Probably with another cat. He's been bitten on top of the head. His whole head hurts—that's why he won't open his eyes or his mouth."

"Will he be okay?" asked Andy.

"Yes," said the doctor. "I think he'll be okay."

"Come to think of it," said Andy's grandma, "I saw a big old brute sneaking out of your yard when I came over yesterday morning."

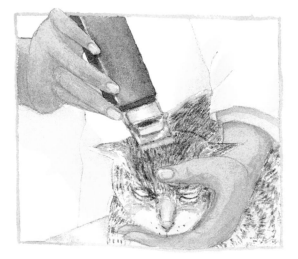

The doctor carefully shaved the fur from around
Frank's wound. After that, no one could bear to look,
but when it was all over, Frank had a tidy white
bandage wrapped around his head. His eyes were
open, but he did not seem to be happy just yet.

"Mom," said Andy, "did your arm
hurt the whole time it was broken?"
"No," said his mom.

"I got used to it. I had
to sleep a certain way.

"I had to try to write
with my left hand.

"When the bandage came off, my arm looked really skinny and pale. I was a little bit afraid to use it at first.

"But pretty soon it looked normal, and I didn't think about it at all."

And that's how it happened with Frank, the cat, too.

The Er

And that's how it happened with Frank.